Disney's
My Very First Winnie the Pooh™
Owl's Trip South

Adapted by
Barbara Gaines Winkelman

Illustrated by
John Kurtz

SCHOLASTIC INC.

New York Toronto London Auckland Sydney
Mexico City New Delhi Hong Kong Buenos Aires

Published by Scholastic Inc., 90 Old Sherman Turnpike, Danbury, CT 06816
by arrangement with Disney Licensed Publishing.

SCHOLASTIC and associated logos are trademarks
and/or registered trademarks of Scholastic Inc.

ISBN 0-7172-8905-2

Printed in the U.S.A.

Owl invited Pooh to his house for tea.

"Pooh," said Owl, "I need to practice an important announcement. I want to make sure that it is perfect."

"I'm glad to help you, Owl," said Pooh.

Owl cleared his throat and declared, "Pooh, I am flying south for the winter."

"Oh," said a very puzzled Pooh. "Does that mean you're leaving us?"

"Just for the winter, Pooh," explained Owl. "I will be back in the spring."

"Oh, bother," Pooh said. "It's going to be lonely here without you, Owl. By the way, exactly how far is this place called South?"

"South is not a place, Pooh," Owl explained. "It is the direction birds fly in the winter."

"Look up in the sky," Owl continued. "You will see groups of birds flying together. They are going south because they are birds. I am a bird. So, as such, I intend to fly south too."

"Excuse me, Owl," began Pooh cautiously. "Exactly *why* do birds fly south for the winter?"

Everyone sat down on a nearby log to listen. Gopher sat in the hole leading down to his tunnel and explained.

"We mussst do sssome hard work," he said. "When we work, we are ssso busy thinking about what we are doing that we forget to be sssad."

"Good idea!" said Rabbit. "Why didn't I think of that? Let's rake leaves!"

Everyone except Tigger went right to work. Tigger played in a leaf pile that Rabbit had made.

"Tigger," scolded Rabbit, "you're messing up my leaf pile!"

"That's the point, buddy-boy!" explained Tigger. "Playing keeps my mind off sad thoughts better than working does."

Tigger looked so happy that even Rabbit had to smile.

"Because they have visitations to make to their relatives in the south," explained Owl. "In my opinion, it is also a good time to go because it is cold up north and warm down south."

"Could a bear also go south for the winter?" inquired Pooh.

"No, Pooh. Notice that bears do not have wings. Therefore, bears are not able to fly and it would take far too long to get there."

By now, Owl was ready to make his announcement to the others. He and Pooh went outside and found Rabbit, Tigger, Piglet, and Eeyore.

"Attention, everyone, please!" Owl began. "In the great tradition of all birds everywhere, I will be going south for the winter. I wish to say good-bye."

"Y-y-you're leaving us?" asked Piglet sadly.

"Just for the winter," answered Owl.

"You're going now, Owl?" asked a very concerned Rabbit. "You need to get organized! Right away! Do you have a map?"

"I do!" said Owl as he spread out his map. "I have planned my route. Let me show you."

"Gosh and golly!" said Tigger. "That map's upside down! It just doesn't look right. What are all those colors?"

Owl turned to Tigger and said, "The blue colorations are water. The green ones are land. I will fly over all of this water and all of this land to get down south."

"Owl!" cried Tigger. "That's too far. We won't be able to see you or talk to you. It's impossibibble!"

"As I said before, I'll be back with the return of seasonal warmth, Tigger. But for now I must go. Good-bye, all! I shall see you in the spring!"

Tigger sighed loudly. "I miss that flyin' fellow already," he said.

"I miss his stories," Piglet sniffed.

Everyone nodded in agreement.

They all started walking home. When they got to Gopher's hole, they told him the sad news about Owl's departure.

"Sssay," whistled Gopher, "I know a perfect sssolution to misssing sssomeone."

"And what is that, Gopher?" asked Pooh.

"Hoo-hoo-hoo-hoo!" Tigger cried as he played in the leaves. Then he saw Gopher giving him a look.

"When I'm finished playing, I'll clean up," Tigger added. "I promise!"

When they had finished raking, Pooh and Tigger wandered down by the stream.

"I've never been without Owl," lamented Tigger. "I never knew how much I would miss him."

They crossed the bridge and sat down together in a quiet place.

"Maybe . . . ," said Pooh, thinking hard, "maybe if you miss Owl so much, and you want him to stop being apart from you, you should go visit him."

"But Pooh," said Tigger, "how would I go? Wouldn't you want to come with me?"

"Well, I'm a bear. Owl told me that bears can't go south because they cannot fly. But perhaps you, Tigger, could bounce?" suggested Pooh.

"Great idea, Pooh-boy!" said Tigger. "Let's see if tiggers can bounce that far!"

As Tigger bounced, he laughed and shouted, "Here I come, Owl!"

He bounced higher and higher. But he couldn't seem to bounce farther and farther. In fact, he kept landing in the same spot right next to Pooh.

Meanwhile, Owl was about to land in the south, or so he thought. He made a turn here, he made a turn there. He wanted to make sure he was traveling in the right direction. He flew around and around for a long time. After a while, everything looked familiar.

"I think I'm going to like it down south," thought Owl.

Suddenly Owl saw some figures in a clearing below.

"The other birds!" he thought. "I must be there already."

As Owl flew closer to the figures, he noticed something familiar about them.

"Look!" Tigger shouted, pointing to the sky. "Owl is back!"

"What a pleasant surprise!" said Owl as he landed. "I didn't expect visitors! How did you get down south so fast?"

"We didn't, Owl," Rabbit explained. "We're here in the Hundred-Acre Wood, right where you started."

"Hoo-hoo-hoo!" laughed Tigger. "Let's celebrate! Let's have a Bird-Day Party for the return of our favorite bird."

So that's exactly what they did. They put on bird costumes and celebrated Owl's return.

"Well, I must say. . . ," declared Owl, beginning his second announcement that day, ". . .it is splendid to be home! Owls, in my opinion, should never go south for the winter, especially when they have all the friends they require right here in the Hundred-Acre Wood."